The
Mariah Delany
Lending Library
Disaster

The
Mariah Delany
Lending Library
Disaster

SHEILA GREENWALD

A YEARLING BOOK

Published by
Dell Publishing Co., Inc.
1 Dag Hammarskjold Plaza
New York, New York 10017

To my sister Lila

Yearling ® TM 913705, Dell Publishing Co., Inc.

ISBN: 0-440-45327-5

Reprinted by arrangement with Houghton Mifflin Company

Printed in the United States of America

March 1986

10 9 8 7 6 5 4 3 2

CW

1

Mariah Delany," her mother said solemnly, "if you would only apply yourself to your school work and your books the way you do to all your enterprises and money-making schemes, you would be at the very top of your class."

Mariah stuck out her lower lip and cut a jelly doughnut in half. This was not the first or even the fiftieth time she had heard her mother offer this particular observation, and the doughnut was far more interesting to contemplate. They were sitting at the kitchen table only six months after the collapse of the Magic Mariah Method for the Harmonica. It was early November. The first report card had just come in and was being held at this moment in Mrs. Delany's hand. The messages from her teachers written on this card all seemed to agree that Mariah Delany "could do better," that Mariah Delany "did not apply herself," that she "somehow resisted books and whatever they had to say." Mrs. Delany and Mariah were going over the comments on this report with a fine-toothed comb. Even sweetening the sour words with sugary doughnuts was not much help.

"I guess you'll make a bigger effort now?" Mrs. Delany asked hopefully. "And try to apply yourself a little more, dear. Let up on all your enterprises and become a student for a change; that's what you should be doing at this time in your life.

After all, you're eleven years old, and not in need of supporting yourself."

Mariah pushed the shaggy no-colored hair behind her oversized ears. With her distant green eyes she observed her mother. She liked her mother, even though Mrs. Delany was hopeless about plans of any kind. A forgetful dreamy lady who wrote long boring articles on writers Mariah had never heard of, Mrs. Delany also taught English at a school on Long Island and seemed cut off from the world by the thickest pair of glasses anybody ever saw. Mariah knew that if anyone was more hopeless at plans and schemes than her mother, it was her father. He could hardly get through a toll booth without putting in too much money. He was a book publisher and he wrote articles that were about as boring as Mrs. Delany's, only they had to do with history. The Delanys' apartment was so crammed with books that you practically had to be a contortionist to walk around them. Mariah had learned not only to walk around them but to avoid them in every way. Right now she could tell her mother was warming up for a BOOK LECTURE. Mariah bit into the half doughnut so that the jelly spilled out all around her tongue, and confectioners' sugar powdered her upper lip and even tickled the inside of her nose. Her mother began to talk. Mariah began to not listen.

Mariah Delany at the age of eleven had a well-established reputation for being enterprising. Enterprising Mariah had introduced a sideline of comics at her lemonade stand the summer she turned ten, causing the three other stands on her street to fold. When two lemonade stands reopened, offering a sideline of comics, Mariah switched to used and broken toys plus a selection of Kool-Aid flavors. Then she took over the other stands as subsidiary branches.

When she was ten and a half, Mariah learned to play "Turkey in the Straw" on the harmonica. The day after she learned this she posted a sign in her school. The sign said that she would offer harmonica lessons on a group or individual basis and that she guaranteed the student would play "Turkey in the Straw" after the first half-hour lesson. Mariah's friend Lea Coopersmith stood in front of the sign playing "Turkey in the Straw" and assuring everyone that she had learned from the Magic Mariah Method for the Harmonica. Twenty-five people signed up for lessons, including the math teacher. Since fifteen of her students had no harmonicas, Mariah consulted a local musical instrument shop and learned that she could get a discount if she ordered fifteen harmonicas. Mariah collected the full price from her students, bought the harmonicas at a discount, and kept the difference.

Her very first student was a small boy

named Clark Bunce. He could not master "Turkey in the Straw" in the half-hour lesson and wanted his money back. Mariah was determined to teach him and make good on her guarantee. She worked with him for two and one-half hours. Finally, even determined, enterprising Mariah had had it. She threw the harmonica at Clark Bunce and hollered, "You idiot! You don't know how to make music; you only make noise." Then she slammed out of his house. As she walked home the thought came to her that she just might have twenty-five Clark Bunces on her hands. She decided very quickly to get out of the harmonica business.

But all these projects were small potatoes, or, as Mariah would say, "peanuts," compared to one that she could not even have imagined on that spring evening walking home from Clark Bunce's.

"Mariah dear, if you'd just get into the

habit of reading, I know you'd love it," Mrs. Delany was saying. The jelly doughnut was nearly gone. Mariah had successfully not listened to her mother for several minutes. "Every day pick up a book for just half an hour. Give it a chance. There are such wonderful things to read."

"Not in our house," Mariah said. "I don't like our books."

Mrs. Delany bit her lip trying to hold back vexation. "All right," she said, suddenly determined. "Finish your doughnut, put on your coat, and come with me."

"Where? "

"To the Public Library, my dear Mariah, where there has *got* to be something you will want to read."

Mariah frowned. There went the afternoon's plans. She had a date with her friend Levine to set up a plant store in the building's outer lobby. Levine's mother, a plant freak, would not mind their taking cuttings and clippings of this and that. Mariah figured that, by sticking them in paper cups, with very little investment they could rake in a possible five dollars. "I have a date."

"Break it," Mrs. Delany said. "You have entirely too many dates, too many schemes, and too many enterprises for an eleven-year-old with terrible grades."

Mariah called Levine on the house phone and told her that if she went ahead on the plant store idea without her, Mariah would never include her in another plan. Then she pulled on her jacket and marched off with her mother to the local branch of the New York Public Library.

2

The library was closed. A white cardboard sign hanging in the glass door announced that, due to cutbacks in the city budget, the library would not open at all on Thursday and would only be open half-days for the rest of the week.

"Why, this is outrageous," Mrs. Delany gasped. She squinted at the sign and registered true anguish. As she often told Mariah, she had spent her entire childhood in the library. It had been her sanctuary,

her refuge, her very favorite place. She went to it every day after school and read and read. Mariah thought that her mother must have been the most out-of-it little nitwit anybody ever knew. She would have probably been embarrassed to know her.

"I guess we'd better go home," Mariah said.

Mrs. Delany tore herself away from the

sign, but on the long walk home she didn't stop talking for a minute. "Do you realize what this means, Mariah? To be locked out of the library like this? What this means for all the children who *love* books and reading? Why, it's a terrible, terrible thing."

Mariah was thinking, "What luck." She could still call Levine and start clipping spider-plant shoots. But when they entered the lobby of their building, Mariah found that Levine had set up the plant business with a little jerk named Mona from the sixth floor, whose mother had contributed four African violets. Mariah was furious. "I warned you," she said.

"I couldn't help it," Levine insisted.

Mariah stormed upstairs, where she was left to roam around the book-crammed apartment. "No TV today," her mother had said.

Mrs. Delany sat at her desk, busily at work. Mariah prowled.

"Haven't you anything to do?" her mother said, slamming her pen down. "A book to read, homework, something?"

Books, books, books, books. Books had ruined the day.

"Okay," Mariah tripped on a stack of unshelved volumes. She flopped on the sofa and picked up one of the tumbled books and looked around her at the piles and piles and shelves and shelves of them. She was surrounded. And then it hit her. The best idea she had ever had in her life. Immediately, Levine's plants withered in her mind. Plants were for anybody.

This new idea had everything. It filled a crying need, if her mother was right. It involved practically no investment. She had the market and she had the goods.

Mrs. Delany looked up. "Why, Mariah! You look positively radiant. Did you finally find a good book?"

"I found many good books," Mariah beamed. "And I *love* them all."

"How nice," Mrs. Delany said. Her eyes glowed like mellow candle flames behind the thick circles of tinted glass.

3

That night Mariah was in the first full fever of her enterprising plan-making. She would go to the library the very next day to check on a few things, observe the librarian in action, and take notes on what she saw. She wanted to be sure to do things right and not make an amateurish, sloppy hash out of such a potentially good scheme. She also had to decide whether to take in partners or to work alone. Levine was out; an untrustworthy type. However, on the second floor of her building there was a boy named Something-or-other Pollack, Joe maybe, who looked reliable. Coopersmith was a possibility though she didn't live in the building, and a building associate could come in handy for this enterprise. Finally, Mariah decided to settle the personnel problems later. At dinner she was so preoccupied, she could hardly eat. Aside from her parents, Mariah's family included her brother, Irwin, who was in high school. Irwin, a regular book-reading Delany, was their parents' pride and joy. Mariah had already concluded that when she grew up she would probably have to support Irwin. Every time he went out on the street Irwin either got lost or lost his money. No one even had to rip Irwin off; he managed to get separated from his money all by himself. However, he had the sort of grades that cause envy. He was at the top of every class and his scores had wings. He was Super Student, equally good at every subject, a fact that seemed unbelievable to Mariah. The Delanys thought Irwin was just about perfect. They had no idea, however, what to make of Mariah, and sometimes seemed a little scared of her.

"And so what did my girl do today?" Mariah's father asked as the stew was being ladled out.

"We went to the library, me and Mom."

Henry Delany practically ignited, he glowed so. "The library! Why Mariah, how fine."

"It was closed, Henry," Mrs. Delany said in tragic tones. "Closed. I know we read about these awful budget cuts in the newspaper, but when you stand there in front of the closed door, it all becomes horribly real. Locked — a building full of wonderful books that should be available to children and adults, that *were* available to me and to you every day. Every day I ran to the library, my favorite place in all the world. The library was where I learned about

17

books and the miracles of stories, fairy tales, and, later, novels. The library was where the seeds of all my work were planted. When I think of how children today are to be denied what I had, I cannot believe it."

"Terrible, terrible." Mr. Delany nodded. "Whom can we write to or call?"

"The mayor, the governor, the city councilmen," Mrs. Delany intoned.

"Jerks," Mariah thought. Didn't they know that all those letters went into a big trash can or got answered by a computer? She had sent just such a letter off last year to the mayor. It had to do with an idea she had for garbage collection. When she got a reply, she made sure to rub the mayor's signature with a wet finger. The ink didn't budge. A form letter from beginning to end. She pushed a piece of bread around her dish to sop up gravy.

"Mariah's first reports came today." Mrs. Delany switched the subject alarmingly.

"Mmm." Mr. Delany looked up. "How's it going?"

"The same."

Mr. Delany sighed. "Of course, we all know that when the day comes when Mariah decides to invest the kind of time and energy she uses up in her enterprises on her school work, she'll be an A-plus student."

"I don't want to be an A-plus student," Mariah said.

This remark drew Irwin's head out of his dish. "You don't?"

"No, I don't."

Irwin ducked back into his stew, and shook his head in disgust.

After the stew, Mariah could not wait to get into her room so that she could start some specific planning. She always loved this first phase of any brainstorm.

"Don't you want any dessert dear?" Mrs. Delany called as Mariah bolted from the table.

"Unh-unh. I have loads of work to do."

"Oh, Mariah, that's wonderful," and then, more softly, to her husband, "You know Henry, I really think something happened this afternoon that changed Mariah's entire point of view about books and learning. I saw her suddenly looking at our own collection, as if seeing it for the very first time. She was on fire. It was beautiful to see. She actually said she loved books. You know how she has never had any interest in them whatsoever. "Perhaps . . ." Mrs. Delany put her chin on her palm and stared thoughtfully into her coffee cup. "Perhaps it was that trip to the library, finding it closed and realizing what a gift books are and how not everyone is lucky enough to have them . . . perhaps that did it."

"Mmmmmm, maybe," Mr. Delany lit up his pipe.

Mariah closed her door and restrained herself from guffawing. "Okay," she said out loud. "First thing, I've got to set it up." She began to write on the back of her notebook. "I need pockets in each book for the cards, then I need cards." She chewed on her lower lip as she wrote, thinking of more and more things that were needed. Soon her list filled a page and a half . . . glue, Scotch tape, shoebox for card catalogue . . . masking tape, rubber stamp

21

with date and ink pad, and, of course, that trip to the library to see exactly how they operated.

At ten-thirty Mrs. Delany poked her head into the room. "Still working, Mariah? Oh my."

"I had a lot to do," Mariah sat at her desk in her pajamas, bent over her notebook. "By the way, Mom, tomorrow I'll be a little late coming home. I'm going to the library direct from school."

Mrs. Delany nearly fell over. "You are? Oh, Mariah, how nice. How terrifically nice."

"It sure is," Mariah said.

"Good night." Mrs. Delany blew a kiss, and giggled to herself. "This is just unbelievable."

"Good night," Mariah said. When the door had closed she thought to herself, "Yes, unbelievable for now anyway." The Mariah Delany Lending Library was still but a dream in the mind of its creator.

4

The next day was Friday. Mariah bounded out of bed and got dressed for school. The school she attended was medium-sized and eight blocks to the south of their building, facing Central Park. This school had appeared to be very informal and casual, but Mariah had soon learned not to trust appearances. In fact, it seemed to Mariah that her teachers constantly demanded perfect work, and if they didn't get it, they never stopped breathing down your neck.

Mariah's neck had been breathed down, till it felt like a wind tunnel, by more teachers than she cared to remember. Surprisingly, this did not prevent Mariah from liking school. Many of her enterprises could never have gotten off the ground without school. She had run a juice concession in the fourth grade, but had been forced to close it down for sanitary reasons. In third grade she had set up a frame service for the art work of first- and second-graders. Using school masking tape (no investment), she got three cents a frame. Also she had sold old gum cards, mittens, and stickers through school connections. Mariah had enlisted many good associates at school. Aside from Coopersmith, there were Suzy Bellamy and Emma Pinkwater. As she brushed her teeth, Mariah was considering which, if any, of these should be included in her fantastic new enterprise.

"Good morning, Mariah dear," Mrs. Delany sang as Mariah flopped onto a kitchen chair. "How sweet you look this morning."

Mariah wondered if her mother could see her at all through those jam jars over her eyes.

"I know you're going to school this morning well prepared. Isn't it a nice feeling, dear?"

"Uh-huh."

"When you get used to that nice feeling of doing your work and being prepared, you'll never want to go back to the other way, Mariah."

"Uh-huh."

"I just have a feeling your reports will be very different from now on."

"Yup." Mariah bit into a bagel and chewed and chewed. It wasn't that she didn't love her mother. She loved her very much. However, she felt the same way about her as she felt about Irwin; both could hardly cross the street by themselves. Mariah knew that though Gertrude Delany had wonderful book knowledge and very high standards, neither she nor her husband had any business sense at all. Mariah had realized this several years before when she had taken the trouble to train several caterpillars she'd found in the country to answer to their names. She had carefully brought these caterpillars back to the city to sell as trained caterpillars. When the Delanys got wind of what she was doing, they made her return the money she had received, and lectured her on ethics. They told her that she knew full well that those caterpillars didn't know their names, and that what she was doing was dishonest. Mariah didn't argue with them on this issue, but she quietly continued to believe that if people wanted to think there was such a thing as a trained caterpiller and were willing to pay for it, they should be entitled to do so without any meddlesome bookworm Delany interfering.

So she chewed her bagel and "uh-huhed"

and "yupped" until her happy, misguided mother kissed her off to school with an extra tug on the muffler.

In school Mariah decided to tell Pinkwater, Coopersmith, and Bellamy that something big was in the works, but could not be talked about just yet. This news got the three girls very worked up.

"Why don't you tell?" Pinkwater wanted to know at lunch. "I mean, what's the secret for?" Emma Pinkwater was tremendously tall. She was already bigger than anyone in sixth grade — boy, girl, or teacher — and she was still growing. In spite of her size she was timid and given to awful spates of slouching, mumbling, and tearfulness.

"I always told you all *my* plans right away, Mariah," she mumbled sulkily.

"Yeah, and they weren't worth much."

"Pinkwater's right," Suzy Bellamy said. "I bet you don't have any plans."

"Teasing won't work," said Mariah.

"You'll just have to wait and see." She gathered up her paper bag, sandwich wrappings, and empty container and left the table with a confident lift of her chin. She kept the secret all day, and by leaving school immediately upon dismissal, managed to avoid walking with any of her friends, or being followed by them.

She did exactly what her mother had done as a girl. She ran to the library as soon as school was out. The seven blocks were traversed in fewer minutes, and Mariah appeared at the children's reading room in a breathless, excited state.

"My word," the librarian behind the desk remarked, "you were certainly in a rush to get here."

"Yes indeed," Mariah agreed. "Now, how do I get a card?"

The librarian seemed delighted by Mariah's interest and intensity; she looked as if she would die if she didn't get a card.

"First of all, catch your breath, and then

step this way." They walked to the other end of the long desk. The librarian had a nice face, with wide-set gray eyes and a pleasant smiling mouth. "Have you ever had a card?"

"Yes, but I lost it."

"Okay, then, fill out this card and I'll give you a temporary one till the new card comes in the mail. That way, you'll be able to take out books today."

Mariah filled in the card.

"Very good," said the librarian, reading

over the card. "Now you just have a nice time looking around, Mariah, and if you need any help finding something, don't hesitate to ask."

Mariah walked a few paces from the desk, pulled out a low stool, sat down on it, and positioned herself so that she could observe how books were returned and withdrawn. She certainly didn't need the machine the library used to photograph the borrower's card and the book's card. A simple rubber stamp with the date on it would suit her library just as well. After she had satisfied herself on this point she strolled slowly up and down the aisles, occasionally jotting down a note to herself in her notebook. Then she opened a few books and inspected them thoroughly: the envelopes inside, the cards, the covers, the stamps. Then she examined paperbacks, magazines, picture books, and the card catalogue. When she had done all this and was satisfied, she wrapped the muffler around her neck, put on her mittens, and prepared to leave.

"Oh, Mariah," the librarian called after her just as she was going out the door, "didn't you find a single book you wanted?"

"Not really," Mariah said.

"Well, my goodness, you were so eager, I thought you'd walk out with half the collection. What were you looking for?"

"I was, uh, just looking to see how you operate."

"How we operate?" The librarian was amazed. "What do you mean? Do you want to be a librarian?"

"Sort of," said Mariah.

"My name is Lizzy Phipps and if I can be of any assistance, let me know." Lizzy Phipps put out her hand for shaking and looked very amused.

"Sure thing," Mariah said, wishing to be gone. She had masses of work to do. As she ran down the steps of the library she thought, "Watch out Lizzy Phipps; here comes the competition."

When Mariah got to the apartment, nobody was home. Mrs. Delany had a full day of teaching on Friday and then stayed late to meet with students. Mariah rejoiced in the empty apartment. First she poured out a large glass of milk, and while drinking it, rummaged around the breadbox, hoping to turn up a leftover cupcake or a box of cookies. Finding nothing in that category, she consoled herself with three slices of toast drenched with butter and sprinkled with cinnamon. Having finished this snack, she cleaned up carefully and washed her hands. One thing Mariah had noticed at the library was that it was a clean and orderly and tidy establishment.

She unpacked the fresh new file cards she had just purchased at the stationery store, and set them on her desk. Then she did a bit of searching in her mother's desk drawers for such items as paper clips, rubber bands, Scotch tape, pencils, and ink pads. She was quickly stocked to meet all her needs. When this was done and Mariah could look with satisfaction and pleasure at her supplies, she went into the living room, where the largest collection of the Delanys' books was kept.

Books, books, books, and books. They were crammed into every inch of space on every shelf. Bookshelves lined every bit of wall space. Books were heaped on the desk and table tops; piles of them rose from the floor, in the corners, and near the bottoms of the shelves, under the piano and on the radiator. Books and books. Mariah rubbed her very clean hands together and grinned.

She referred to the notes she had taken in the library. Categories: Biography, Fiction, Geography, Fairy Tales, Picture Books. She would begin with Biography, as that seemed the easiest to gather since

"Biography" was usually in the title of the book: *The Biography of Helen Keller* or *The Biography of Beethoven*. Using a small stepladder for the higher shelves, Mariah put together a decent Biography section in forty minutes. She carried the books into her room and stacked them on the floor. Then she returned to the living room to fill in the gaps on the shelves with books from the piles on the floor. She happily observed that no spaces could be detected.

After Biography, Mariah assembled her Fiction collection. This was a little more difficult because she didn't know which of all the novels she found would be suitable. She picked out books by authors she had heard of or knew about from school. She chose a set of Dickens because it was so beautifully bound in a rich leather. She also chose Tarkington, Poe, Conan Doyle, and Alcott. Fairy Tales came next and were easier. Like "Biography" the titles helped. For Geography she used some atlases.

By five o'clock she had her initial collection stacked on the floor under her bed. By six, when Irwin came in the door, Mariah had pasted the envelope pockets into half the books and had written, in black Magic Marker, PROPERTY OF THE MARIAH DELANY LENDING LIBRARY across the endpapers and title pages. By seven, when her parents came home, Mariah was beginning on the file card system (two cards for each book in the collection).

"Hello," Gertrude Delany called from the foyer. "We're hoooome."

Mariah came out of her room and closed the door quickly behind her.

"Where did you go this afternoon, Mariah?" Mrs. Delany asked a trifle too casually.

"I told you yesterday," Mariah replied. "To the library."

"Oh, Henry." Mrs. Delany beamed as if all her prayers had been answered. "You see she did, she did. At last our Mariah has found books."

"That's for sure," Mariah said.

5

Over the weekend Mariah stashed the collection in her closet and under the bed, which was unnecessary since Mrs. Delany never quite cleaned up her own room much less anybody else's. She rarely ventured into Irwin's and Mariah's rooms, assuming that Teresa, the weekly cleaning lady, did. Teresa really didn't do much more than tidy the kitchen, polish the silver, and change the linen.

At any rate, everything was going according to plan. Mariah had finished both

the cards and the card catalogue by Sunday night. She really loved her card catalogue. She loved the way she could flip the file cards in the shoebox and look up books by author and title. She had blank spaces for the date of withdrawal and return. She only needed to get a stamp with the date on it and several nice new pencils and a flower to put into a vase on her desk. (She had noticed the nice flowers on Lizzy Phipps's desk.) She would place this vase next to the shoebox with the file cards and a cup full of pencils, and then she would be in business. The only other thing that remained to be done was the clearing out of her bookshelves and the arranging of the collection upon them, complete with labels marking the categories. She would do these things Monday afternoon. However, she had a great deal to do on Monday.

In art class Monday morning, Mariah made her first poster.

THE MARIAH DELANY LENDING LIBRARY

LOCKED OUT AT THE PUBLIC LIBRARY?

BUDGET CUTS GETTING YOU DOWN?

CAN'T FIND YOUR FAVORITE BOOK

WHEN YOU WANT IT?

DON'T DESPAIR

THE MARIAH DELANY LENDING LIBRARY

IS HERE FOR YOUR READING PLEASURE

OPEN WEEKDAY AFTERNOONS

FROM THREE-THIRTY TO FIVE

HOT COCOA SERVED FREE

ON OPENING DAY

Beneath this Mariah wrote her address and drew a small map of the surrounding blocks, marking the route to take from school. She hung up the poster on the bulletin board while Pinkwater and Bellamy looked on.

"So that's it," Pinkwater said. "For crying out loud. Why didn't you tell us?"

"Had my reasons," Mariah said. "If it's a success I'll need some help — more posters and an assistant, maybe."

Pinkwater shrugged, but Bellamy was definitely interested. "Is it a real library, Mariah?"

"Come have a look."

Mariah didn't know whether it was the cocoa or the books, but it seemed everyone came to "have a look." Opening day at the Mariah Delany Lending Library was a complete success. No enterprise of hers had ever gotten off to a stronger start. It surpassed her greatest expectations.

The entire sixth grade of her school arrived, with the exception of Coopersmith, who much to her disgust had an orthodontist appointment.

Teresa was the only one at home (aside from Mariah) when the crowds began to arrive.

"What's going on?" Teresa looked up from the stacks of cutlery she was polishing, as Mariah filled paper cups (left over from the lemonade business) with cocoa.

"Just some kids from school," Mariah said.

"Some kids from school? It looks like the whole entire place to me. You're some popular young lady." Teresa shook her head in wonder.

Mariah's room was packed. Kids on the floor, kids on her bed, kids on the windowsill, two in the closet, and four more in the bathroom. Mariah brought in the cocoa by the trayful. There were empty cups all over. "Does everybody understand how this works?" she asked loudly. "The books are

41

free only if you return them within the two-week period. That's two weeks on the nose. If you go one day over two weeks, it starts costing you. It costs to the tune of two cents per day each day over the two weeks. Now two cents a day is cheaper than the Public Library of New York, and furthermore, I am open *every* weekday afternoon and am unaffected by budget cuts. I give personal attention and feature a homelike atmosphere." These last words reminded Mariah that she had better check the time. Very soon, she figured, Irwin would return to the "homelike atmosphere," not to mention her parents, who well might wonder what was up and ask a lot of questions.

"You've got five minutes to make your selections because the library will be closing."

It was amazing. Everybody chose at least one book. The collection was depleted by more than half. Mariah sat at her desk

with the shoebox in front of her and a vase with a daisy in it just to the side. She wrote out file cards and stamped the date on them and made up duplicates and stamped and filed and smiled at her customers. Soon they were all milling around in the foyer, putting on their jackets, preparing to leave. Almost everyone had gone by the time Mrs. Delany opened the front door and blinked at the last six borrowers, who were about to depart.

"Oh my. Well, hello. I'm Mrs. Delany. Mariah, is this a gathering of some sort?"

"Yes," Mariah said.

"How nice." Mrs. Delany looked a bit concerned. "A social gathering, Mariah? Not some new venture, I trust."

"We have a sort of book club," Mariah whispered.

"That's lovely." Mrs. Delany could hardly believe the good news. "How truly fine."

"So long, Mariah." Bellamy waved. "Are you sure you don't need an assistant yet?"

"A what?" Mrs. Delany asked and whipped out of the coat closet. The word "assistant" had alarmed her.

"Uh, no. Not necessary." Mariah shoved Bellamy out the door, along with the other stragglers.

"Mariah dear." Mrs. Delany waited till

the door was closed behind the last visitor. A worried wrinkle was on her brow. "I really hope you aren't in some sort of enterprise again. I mean, I hope you aren't, you know . . ."

"Wheeling and dealing," Mariah provided.

"Yes, wheeling and dealing. You do know how we feel about that and how we want to see all that wonderful energy channeled into . . . other things."

"That's just what I'm doing, Ma," Mariah said, knowing that "other things" was another way of saying "books." Then she grinned from oversized ear to oversized ear. "Honest."

"Oh, good." Mrs. Delany, smiling and reassured, went to restock her desk, which had so suddenly and mysteriously run out of paper clips, tape, and rubber bands.

6

As the days of the opening week passed, the amazing success of the Mariah Delany Lending Library not only continued but grew. Mariah had to replenish her collection from the living room, hall, study, bedroom, and even the kitchen (she started a Cookbook section). She began to worry that her parents would begin to notice what were now a few real gaping spaces on the shelves. She filled them in as best she could from the stacks on the floor. Once in a while she wondered if what she was doing was dishonest, since she did it in a secretive way, as far as her parents were concerned. However, she decided she was not dishonest because she was not taking anything, merely borrowing. She was simply utilizing a natural resource in the Delany apartment. She had also decided that when the money started to come in, she would give her parents a percentage, perhaps in the form of a gift. At the moment of presenting this gift she would very carefully tell them what she had been doing. In the meantime, even without cocoa, the library was a would-be gold mine. Every day borrowers came, not only from the sixth grade, but from the fifth and seventh and eighth. In order to satisfy the older group, Mariah dipped into her parents collection of sexy books and even made that a category: Sexy Books. In this, she included novels as well as works of anatomy, with a key to the good pages. She took Pinkwater on as an assistant because Pinkwater was a terrific reader and very good at finding specific chapters in books for interested borrowers. Bellamy helped out with the growing card system, and poor little Levine came up one day nearly crying to be let in on it, bearing half the profits from the plant business as a peace offering. Mariah told her she would think it over. Mariah was a very cool operator.

"Mariah," Mrs. Delany said at supper on the Thursday evening of the first brilliantly successful week. "Every day when I come home, there are six or seven children just leaving, and they are all so businesslike. I mean, it doesn't strike me as if you've been having a date or meeting or anything. It's as if . . ." She paused, looking upset. "It's as if you were back in business. What I mean to say, Mariah dear, is, I hope that you are truly trying at school as you said you would, and are not all distracted again. I have a conference next week with

Mrs. Demot, your teacher, but I have always said that I knew as much as I needed to know by observing closely on the home front."

At moments like this, Mariah had to respect her mother for what struck her as weird psychic powers. Mrs. Delany, for all her near-blindness and bookishness, had these flashes of intuition, which set Mariah back several paces and made her sweat. She felt somewhat guilty and had a strong impulse to sit down on her mother's lap and tell her everything. Having a success wasn't much fun if you couldn't share it. But she stopped herself from spilling the beans. This was not the right time, and to tell her parents at the wrong time would get her into nothing but trouble. It could also run the risk of closing down the most ingenious enterprise she'd ever dreamed up. A risk she could not take; not now. So she sucked in her cheeks and bit her tongue and sweated as Mr. Delany gave her a sharp look and exchanged a heavy glance with his wife.

"Mariah," he said slowly, "what's cooking?"

"Nothing." She felt a new pulse in her forehead and wondered if it would show. "Nothing."

"Are you suddenly wildly popular? Why are these groups of kids around every day?"

"It's a club."

"What sort of club?"

"Book."

The magic word. "Ahhhhh."

Both Delanys shelved their misgivings at the sound of that magic word. Dessert was served. Mr. Delany tasted his pudding.

"Gertrude, the pudding is strange."

"I had to put it together from memory, dear. That's why it's a little different."

"Really?"

"I went to look up my recipe in *Best Desserts of the World* and I couldn't find the book. I looked all over for it. It's one of my favorites, and I know I didn't lend it to anyone. I never even let it out of the kitchen."

"Odd."

"Odd isn't the word for it. Though odd would describe this pudding." Mrs. Delany pushed her own dessert away, uneaten. "I can't believe anyone would have pinched that book. This is the kind of thing that makes you believe in goblins."

Henry Delany gave up eating the pudding.

Mrs. Delany went on: "This is one of those things that can drive you right up the wall. My mind keeps dwelling on it. Where, oh where, is my book?"

Mariah had an image of her mother climbing the wall. She decided that cookbooks would have to be one-week deals. She would recall *Best Desserts of the World* immediately. The pudding was terrible. There were a few liabilities to this library business, but she'd straighten them out.

After dinner she had a million things to do: check lists of borrowed books, replenish stock, and so on.

She heard her mother in the kitchen. "Henry, my *Gourmet Tips* is gone. I *must* be going nuts if I misplaced that. This is terrible. I know I had it on the counter."

Mariah closed her door and chewed on a fingernail. She had not thought of the possibility of what was happening now. She figured she had to screw up her courage and tell them, even if she jeopardized everything. She cast a farewell look at her beloved shoebox full of cards, and opened the door.

"Henry, the *Puff Pastry Made Easy Cookbook* is gone, too. If I find out who's responsible for this, I'll . . . I'll murder him."

Mariah closed the door and fell on her bed. She could see now that success was sometimes a lonely and complicated thing.

7

By the end of the second week Mariah was less nervous. Soon the first batch of borrowed books would be coming in, and if not, the money profits would begin to flow. This promise of money cheered her up. How she loved the sound of change jingling in her pockets. How happy it made her to hear it there and to know that when she walked into a shop she could price things and really consider buying them. Her parents, when they had observed this delight she took in having money, were alarmed.

"Whom did she get it from, Gertrude?" her father had once asked. "We, who care so little for material things, who value the mind and the intellect, have produced a child who cares only for the purse, for money, and the things it can buy."

"She's a materialist; let's face it." Mrs. Delany had sighed dramatically. "Let's hope it's a phase and she'll outgrow it."

But Mariah did not think she was a materialist. She didn't compete with other girls over clothes and possessions. She just enjoyed the game of figuring out ways of making money. She enjoyed knowing that she could make money and have it if she liked. She considered herself to be a business person. When she was in the middle of an enterprise she experienced a pleasure and excitement that she got from nothing else. Once her grandfather had told her how he had gone to work at the age of twelve to support his widowed mother and four brothers. He had sold hankies on the street and then saved to rent a store. He told her the story so that she would know about his hard childhood. But Mariah had envied him. How she would love to go out and make the family's money. Then her parents would be grateful and would appreciate her enterprising talents. They would not complain about her. When she had told her grandfather how she felt, he had looked astonished and said, "Why, Mariah, you are a businesswoman." Which was exactly what she wanted to be.

The third week of the Lending Library began without a single book's being returned, including *Best Desserts of the World* and *Gourmet Tips*, which Mrs. Delany seemed to talk about and hunt for several times a day. At first Mariah was delighted because each day a book was overdue meant money. But as the days went by the collection dwindled. No books came in and more books were borrowed. Mariah became apprehensive. Finally she posted an announcement in school, saying that there could be no more borrowing by those who had not returned books.

That did it. No one came to borrow and no one came to return. The Mariah Delany Lending Library was dead as a doornail. Over one hundred and fifty books were gone and not a penny had come in. Mariah was frantic.

"Pinkwater." She cornered her tall friend in school. "Why don't you return your books?"

"Oh gosh, Mariah, I keep forgetting."

"Every day you forget costs you."

"I don't know how to tell you this, Mariah. I feel just terrible, but I don't know what happened to them. Last night I looked and looked. I think they're just lost."

"JUST LOST? What's that supposed to mean?" Mariah yelped.

"Well some person, I won't mention any name, was seen *gift* wrapping one of your precious books."

"Gift wrapping? You mean to give away?"

"Draw your own conclusions, but I think it's a lot worse than their just being lost."

Mariah's heart thudded and sank.

Later, in the lunch room, Pinkwater pretended not to see Mariah and sat down at a distant corner table.

On the lunch line, Mariah grabbed Bellamy. "You'd better return my books," she said.

"But I'm right in the middle."

"Then you have to pay."

"But I don't get an allowance. I can't pay."

"Then return the books right away, and you'll owe me."

"But Mariah, I'm your friend."

Mariah didn't answer her, and Bellamy joined Pinkwater at the corner table.

In the middle of the third week Henry Delany called from the living room to his wife, who was preparing dinner in the kitchen. "Gertrude, my Dickens collection is *gone*. I can't believe it. It was right here. It's always been right here. I just went to look up something in *Great Expectations* and it's gone. They're all gone."

"Along with my *Best Desserts*, and *Gourmet Tips* and *Puff Pastry*."

"This is incredible. I couldn't have misplaced the entire set, Gertrude. Those books are very valuable. They're a special limited edition, worth a small fortune."

"We really should be better organized about our books," Mrs. Delany said. "Perhaps this is a lesson to us. We must arrange them better and make lists of what we've got."

"But I was certain about the Dickens. It was right here." Henry Delany scratched his scalp and looked miserable.

Mariah's stomach turned right over.

This was the first time an enterprise of hers had resulted in such horrendous problems. How did a lending library get its books back? Obviously she did not have the proper technique and obviously she was involved up to the eyeballs. In fact, as she sat on the edge of her bed contemplating her library problems, as well as all the homework she had let slide due to business affairs, her entire throat began to lock off and something like tears could be felt to rise up, though she managed to hold them back. Mariah was no crier. However, she was fast getting into a really bad mess and she needed help. Whom could she turn to? Her mother? Murder had been mentioned. Her father would surely share her mother's point of view after he heard what had become of his priceless set of Dickens. Irwin wouldn't understand. Her grandfather was in Florida.

At dinner everything got worse. "That set of Dickens was probably worth more than anything we own, Gertrude. Though not actually a first edition it's damn close. You know, I wonder if it was stolen."

Mrs. Delany looked at her husband sympathetically. "I just can't imagine how that would have happened, dear. There's been no evidence of anyone's breaking in. My jewelry and the silver are untouched. Would anybody have gone to the trouble to sneak into our apartment and filch a set of Dickens?"

"You thought your cookbooks had been stolen," Henry Delany reminded her.

"So I did," Mrs. Delany admitted. "At the time I couldn't think of any other way they could have left my kitchen. They're so much a part of my life, those books. I reach for them without even thinking, to find out how many eggs or what to set the oven for. Not finding them in their proper place is like not finding a trusted part of myself."

"I know what you mean exactly." Henry Delany looked truly mournful. "A part of

oneself. You don't realize how important these things have become, and what they mean to you until you've lost them." He looked over at Mariah and smiled. "We've called Mariah a materialist, and here we are, hopelessly, helplessly attached to our books. Why, if I knew who took my Dickens, I'd wring his neck."

Mrs. Delany reached over and patted her husband's hand soothingly. Then she noticed Mariah's dish. "Mariah, aren't you hungry? You haven't touched your food."

"I don't feel good."

"Why don't you go and lie down? Perhaps it's all the work you've been doing lately." Mrs. Delany's tone was so sweet and understanding that Mariah could hardly stand it.

She went into her room and curled up on her bed. Inside herself she felt a great black space gathering. "Oooooo," Mariah whimpered. "I need help, somebody." Then she thought of Lizzy Phipps and began to feel a little better. Better enough, at least, to fall asleep.

8

___

Lizzy Phipps remembered Mariah. "There you are, the one who couldn't find a single book. How have you been?"

"Terrible." Mariah leaned over the desk. She had barely made it through the day. No one had returned a single book. Dave Peterson told her he had lost *Great Expectations*, but would gladly give her a paperback copy of it as a replacement.

"A paperback?" Mariah had gasped. She could just imagine what her father would think if he found a paperback in place of his beloved almost-first edition. "You're out of your mind," she said. "The copy you lost was very, very valuable."

"Aw, come off it," Dave said. "It was one of those fancy-looking jobs you can pick up at any secondhand place for a few bucks."

"That's not true," Mariah said. "It was the real thing."

"Who says?"

"My father."

"Your father doesn't know in his entire head what my mother knows in her pinkie about books."

Mariah was so exasperated she was temporarily speechless. Finally she told Dave that her father "lived, breathed, and practically ate" books. "He's a publisher of them, you idiot."

"And my mother . . ." Dave smiled like somebody with a handful of aces. ". . . is a dealer in old, rare, and valuable books."

"You showed her that book?" asked

Mariah. A dark suspicion had begun to grow in back of her mind. She watched Dave carefully.

His cheeks colored. "Uh, not really showed her. She saw it last week, before I lost it, and she said it was one of those cheap flashy jobs, imitation leather and gilt. So, anyway Mariah, I'll replace it with this neat Penguin version, which is probably worth more."

Mariah had run to the library all the way from school. She had hardly eaten since lunch the day before. That afternoon somewhere in the school her mother was having a parent-teacher conference with Mrs. Demot. The jig was definitely up.

Lizzie Phipps stopped smiling. She seemed to recognize that there was something truly awful going on in the depths of the soul of Mariah Delany. "What is it?" she said.

"What do you do in a library," Mariah

blurted, "if nobody brings back the books?" To her surprise and mortification, the mere act of unburdening herself to another person was going to make her start to cry. But she could not stop talking. "If they borrow and borrow and take all the books (gulp) and say they'll bring them back and then they aren't even my . . . the library's books and it turns out that they're practically priceless (gasp) and nobody brings them back or even pays you and somebody saw somebody *gift wrap* one of them and what do you do?" Mariah was crying hard. She let Lizzy Phipps escort her to a chair in the (thank heavens) empty reading room and she let her bring a glass of water and she let her hold a Kleenex to her eyes.

"Mariah, have you gone and opened your own library?"

Mariah nodded. "Lending library," she corrected, and then in a feeble small voice added, "the Mariah Delany Lending Library."

"And so you loaned lots of books?"

Mariah nodded again.

"And not one has been returned?"

More nodding.

"They are well past due and they aren't strictly speaking your books?"

Nod, nod, nod.

"Mariah, you have a problem. "

Mariah buried her face in her two hands.

"But we will figure something out. Did you keep records?"

"Yes."

"You know exactly who took what book?"

Nod.

"I won't ask where you got the books, Mariah, but I suggest that you toughen your collection techniques."

"I asked and asked. People won't even eat lunch with me anymore."

"I'm afraid that's the price you pay. It will get even worse, but you'll find out who your friends are."

"I found out. I don't have any friends." Mariah began to sob again.

"Of course you do. Only it's a little embarrassing for them now. They'll shape up. You'll have to go to work on it. You can start by writing a firm letter explaining the whole thing."

"I'm not a good letter-writer," Mariah said.

"I'll help you with it, then. Come." She took Mariah to her desk, where she picked up paper and pencils. Then she settled her at one of the round library tables. There were books spread out on the table. One of them was *Great Expectations*. The sight of it made Mariah shudder. One of the priceless Dickens. She wondered what was so priceless about it and opened the book. She began to read. It seemed pretty good. Good enough for her to want to turn the page.

"You can read later," Mrs. Phipps said. "Now it's time to write tough letters." She

sat down beside Mariah and pushed the pencil and paper in front of her. "Write down what I say." Lizzy Phipps cleared her throat and looked into space. "According to our records your borrowed book has not been returned to this library and is overdue. Will you kindly return the above as soon as possible so that we do not need to turn this problem over to our collecting agent."

Mariah was writing furiously. "Who,"

she asked, looking up, "is our collecting agent?"

"We'll get to that when the time comes and let's hope that it won't come. Make copies of this letter and give them by hand to every person who has an overdue book. Then see what happens."

"Okay." Mariah folded up the letter and put it in her knapsack.

"Now go home and start writing."

Mariah got up wearily. She felt empty and weak and sick at heart. She looked down at the table. "Oh, can I take this with me?" She picked up the copy of *Great Expectations*.

On the walk home, she realized that she would never write the letters. The whole idea seemed pointless to her. People had come to her house and had taken books with an agreement to return them. They had broken that agreement and now she was going to write a letter? Ridiculous.

Baloney. Mariah's despair began to turn to rage, and as soon as that happened she got hungry. She stopped in and had a pizza, and as she ate she got madder. The madder she got, the more stupid the letter idea seemed. She was too mad to write. What was that about a collecting agent anyway? What collecting agent? She washed down the last bit of pizza crust with a grape soda. She had gotten into this thing and she'd get out of it. Mariah grabbed her book bag and stuffed *Great Expectations* into it. She picked herself up and struck off to Pinkwater's.

Mariah Delany, Collecting Agent.

9

Oh," Pinkwater said when she opened the door to Mariah. "Hi."

"Hi." Mariah gave a half-wave. "I came to get the books back."

"I don't know how to tell you this, Mariah, but I lost them someplace."

"I don't know how to tell you this, Emma Pinkwater, but we're going to find them." Mariah pushed past her into the foyer.

"Listen, Mariah, they're only a week past due, for heaven's sake."

"Well, that's one week too much."

Emma Pinkwater followed Mariah back to the room she shared with her sister. "What are you going to do?" she squeaked.

Mariah was pulling out drawers and heaving things out of them at random. "Find my books."

"I told you I don't know where . . . Oh, Mariah, stop. My sister will kill me. Wait a minute. I think I put them someplace in my desk." Pinkwater was running all around the room in a frenzy, her long legs climbing over the beds and onto a chair and down. "Oh, puh-lease stop making such a mess."

Mariah had just toppled a huge stack of comics from Emma's desk. They slithered all across the bed and floor, and there at the very bottom of the stack were the two borrowed library books.

"Oh, look, Mariah. I had no idea they were at the bottom of that pile of stuff. What luck."

Mariah grabbed the books. "Maybe one day I'll be able to call you a friend again, Emma Pinkwater, but at this moment you are definitely off my list."

"Oh Mariah." Emma fluttered and folded. "What can I do?"

"Nothing." Mariah stormed out of the room. "You're an untrustworthy person."

"I didn't intend to be. I thought I'd lost them, Mariah."

As she opened the door Mariah had an idea. She paused and turned on her heel. Pinkwater was slouched miserably a few paces behind her. "If you mean it about doing something, Emma, I will perhaps consider taking you on as my collecting agent."

"What's a collecting agent?" Emma looked suspicious.

"You'll go around doing what I just did, collecting the books for the Lending Library from other kids."

"Oh no," Emma wailed. "I couldn't."

"I'll think about it, but I make no promises," Mariah said, disregarding Emma's reaction. She opened the door and got out fast.

The walk home was invigorating. True, she had forgotten to collect a cent from Emma, but at least she'd gotten two books back, one of them a Dickens, and she had dreamed up a plan for Pinkwater to go to work for her. These things buoyed up her spirits right to the moment when she opened her own door.

As Mariah took off her jacket, Mrs. Delany approached from the living room. "Mariah, I had a conference with Mrs. Demot."

How could she have forgotten? She looked at her mother's face. BIG TROUBLE.

"Let's sit down, Mariah." Mrs. Delany had never sounded quite this somber. Her lectures were usually of the I'm-sure-you-understand-and-will-do-better variety. But now her long narrow face seemed pinched, and behind the glasses there was real distress in her eyes. "Mariah, Mrs. Demot says that your work has not improved one bit in the past two weeks. I felt such a fool. I started off telling her what a great change had taken place in you and how you are working in a steady and orderly way. She looked at me as if I were mad, Mariah. She said that if anything, your school work has fallen off and you seem preoccupied by some new project. She wasn't sure what."

Mariah rubbed her sweaty palms on her knees and stared at what seemed to her to be a gaping hole on the bookshelf where the Dickens collection had been.

"Oh, Mariah." Mrs. Delany raised hurt and unhappy eyes to her daughter's face. "Have you been deceiving us all along about your new-found love of books? Were you putting us on?"

"No," Mariah said. "It's true. I did have a new-found interest in books." When she said this she felt rotten. She vowed to herself that as soon as all the books were safely back on the shelves she would tell her parents everything, come what may. She just couldn't tell them now. They'd worry themselves sick that she'd never get the books back. She would spare them that worry and at the same time spare herself the horrendous job of telling them at this awful point.

"Can you please help me to understand what you have been doing, Mariah?" Mrs. Delany asked. "I want to know because I want to help. I can't help if I don't understand."

When confronted with questions like this, Mariah's usually active mind went completely numb. She chased frantically around her head for some suitable answer. "I just, uh. I can't seem . . . Well, I enjoy reading the books, but I get carried away and then I don't have time for my school work."

Mrs. Delany's face melted in a sympathetic smile.

Hooray. Mariah knew she had said the right thing.

"I understand so well what you are saying. I always had that very same problem. I'd read and forget everything. I could never put a book down once I started it. I would forget school work, dinner, everything. After lights were supposed to be out,

I'd turn on my flashlight and start reading." Mrs. Delany's face grew soft and pink
at the recollection. Mariah was touched by
the depth and intensity of her mother's
feelings. Mrs. Delany clasped and un-
clasped her hands and smiled and twin-
kled, remembering those precious nights of
reading. Her enthusiasm about books was
almost catching, as was the delight she
radiated when talking about them.
Mariah, who had just gone to the Public

Library for a bit of peace and comfort herself, did not see her mother as a "jerk," right now.

"Why, Mariah, if I'd known how you felt, I could have explained to Mrs. Demot."

"Yeah, but I should learn to manage my reading and my school work better," Mariah said virtuously.

"You're very mature to understand that, Mariah. Our talk has made me confident that you will begin to put all these things together from now on. You are a very special person."

Home free. Mariah sighed. Everything was okay, at least for the time being.

Mrs. Delany got up. "I'd best start dinner. I'll explain to Daddy about Mrs. Demot's report." She paused and looked back shyly at her daughter. "Mariah, I think we had such a good talk." She gave Mariah a small hug and went off happily to the kitchen.

Mariah had to restrain herself from running after her mother and telling her everything. She experienced a new low in feeling rotten. She improved her spirits a little when she returned Emma Pinkwater's books to the shelf and even more when she dialed Pinkwater's number to inform her that she had decided to appoint her the Official Collecting Agent for the Mariah Delany Lending Library. Emma, who was usually delighted to be appointed anything by Mariah, was not delighted.

"I don't want everybody to hate me," she muttered.

"You are the very first person I asked," Mariah said, trying to make the job sound like an honor. "I asked you because I trust you and I think you can do a good job. Anyway, did you hate me when I collected your books?"

"No," said Pinkwater.

"Okay, so what are you worried about?"

The conversation went on for a while, with Mariah exerting more and more pressure and Pinkwater finally agreeing, though not exactly thanking Mariah for the "honor."

By the time she hung up the phone, it was time to set the table and wash up for dinner. Henry Delany had come home. He was sitting in the living room, sipping sherry and reading something. He called to Mariah as she arranged plates and napkins in the dining room. "Mother told me about the good talk you two had, Mariah. You may end up as one of the Delany Bookworms after all." He chuckled delightedly at this thought.

Mariah had returned to the kitchen to fetch the plates when she heard her father call out, "Gertrude, for heaven's sake! One of the missing Dickens books is back on the shelf, exactly where it has always been. I'd swear it wasn't here yesterday."

"Maybe Teresa dusted it and put it down someplace and forgot and then put it back," Mrs. Delany called from the kitchen.

Mariah went to the kitchen door, from where she could see her father standing by the living room shelf holding the returned book lovingly in his hands. Suddenly, just as he opened the volume, she remembered with a sinking feeling that she had forgotten to remove the pocket and card.

There was a terribly long long moment when everything in the apartment seemed to stop, and then Henry Delany roared, "What the hell is the Mariah Delany Lending Library?"

Gertrude Delany looked up from the pot of rice she was fluffing with a fork. She blinked. Then her magnified soft brown eyes fell upon Mariah with immediate understanding.

"Oh Mariah." She sighed, a deep and disappointed sigh.

Harmonicas had been a fizzle. This Lending Library was a Disaster.

10

It was a very rough time Mariah had that night. In fact, once again she found she was too upset to eat her dinner. She really loved her parents and she felt that she had betrayed them. What made it worse was that they didn't say much about it. Henry Delany sat with an expression of real pain in his eyes. He asked Mariah if she had lent many books and if the rest of the Dickens collection was out.

Mariah told him it was, and then

brought in her card catalogue and the shoebox so that her parents could see exactly how many books were involved and where they had gone. Even though they were miserable, they were impressed by her organization and enterprise. She did not inform them that the books were all overdue and that nobody had made a move to return them. In fact, she went out of her way to reassure them that soon all the books would be back on the Delany shelves, safe and sound. Her parents were not reassured. They looked sad and upset and, worst of all, not angry. This lack of anger bothered Mariah more than anything. She wished they would yell and scream, even punish her, but they were too distressed to bother.

Mariah went to bed, but certainly not to sleep. She lay awake thinking for the first time about where being "enterprising" had gotten her. She even made a solemn vow. She promised that if she got back all the books she would really knuckle down and devote her time to her school work and not engage in enterprising ventures of any sort until her grades were up and everybody was pleased with her. This vow gave her some comfort and provided her troubled mind with enough peace so that she could go to sleep.

The next afternoon, walking home from school, Mariah saw Dave Peterson and his mother just half a block in front of her. She began to run, determined to nab him and

make a heavy pitch for her book in front of his book-dealer mother.

"Dave," she called out. She knew he heard her because he began to speed up as if he were trying to get away, but his mother nudged him and turned around.

"David dear, someone is calling you."

"Oh, hi." Dave shrugged. "Hi, Mariah, uh, we're going to get me a pair of shoes."

"I just wondered if my *Great Expectations* showed up."

"Why David!" Mrs. Peterson blinked. "Don't you introduce me to your friends?"

"Oh, meet Mariah Delany," Dave said unenthusiastically.

"We're in kind of a rush, Mariah dear," Mrs. Peterson said. "Saturday we are celebrating our anniversary with a big party and I did so want David to have a new pair of shoes. Today is the only day we can shop."

Dave seemed to be drowning in a sea of mortification.

"But I need to talk to Dave about my book."

"Your book?" Mrs. Peterson looked confused.

"The copy of *Great Expectations* you told him wasn't worth much."

"*I* told him wasn't worth much?" Mrs. Peterson had become a parrot. "My dear, I must confess I don't know what you're talking about but it's been nice meeting a classmate of David's." She was backing away almost as fast as her son.

"I have got to talk to you about my books," Mariah called to the two figures who were by this time running across the street.

For the three days after this incident Mariah tried to collect in earnest. She realized that Pinkwater was doing a terrible job. Nobody took her seriously. If there was to be any collecting, she would have to do it herself. But when she started to collect she found she was received with embarrassment, excuses, and delay. Sometimes there was even ill will. One thing there wasn't was a single returned book. Most of her schoolmates tried to avoid her. When she pinned them down, they fumbled in their book bags, grabbed at their foreheads, and said, "Oh Lord, I forgot, but I'll *definitely* remember tomorrow." Somebody named Jenny Popkin snidely referred to Mariah as "The Collecting Agent," and got a laugh out of a small group in the lunch room.

Mariah cornered Bellamy. "Who did you see gift wrapping one of my books?"

"I didn't see him myself."

"Who is it?"

"I really couldn't say." Bellamy looked at a faraway place over Mariah's shoulder.

Mariah's heart sank. This was the first time she had been avoided by her schoolmates. Even her gang — Pinkwater, Coopersmith, and Bellamy — looked the other way when they saw her coming. After school on Friday she decided it was time for a consultation with Lizzy Phipps.

She dug her hands deep into her pockets and hunched her chin down into her collar and passed a group of classmates on the corner. Some turned away and some stared back until she crossed the street.

"How's it going, Mariah?" Lizzy Phipps asked.

"Lousy," Mariah said. "My folks know. They're in shock. The kids at school won't return the books. They hate me."

"I wish I had the time to talk to you right now, Mariah," said Lizzy Phipps, "but as you can see I've got twenty zillion things to do." She was pushing a cart of unshelved books around the reading room, returning them to their proper places. She lurched to a halt and clapped a hand to her forehead. Idea! "Hey, Mariah, I just thought of something. You could help me out. These budget cuts are murder and I'm always short-handed. How about your joining the system for a while and giving me a hand in *my* library?"

"What do you mean?" Mariah was actually sick to death of the very word "library."

"I mean shelve these books for me. At this point, with your own experience you know all about categories and alphabetizing. Tell me when you're finished."

"Well, I . . ." Mariah was looking around for a way out, but Lizzy Phipps had more or less pushed the cart at her and run back to her desk.

Mariah shelved the books carefully, even taking pleasure in completing the job quickly. The work took her mind off her problems. Just as she replaced the last book, Lizzy Phipps ran up to her with one of the *Curious George* books in her hand. "Would you please read this story to that group of children, Mariah, before they wreck the place?"

Mariah settled herself on a low stool in the Picture Book section, with *Curious George* on her knee. A circle of small children formed around her. They listened to every word, and when she finished they pleaded for more. She read them *Madeline* next. She held up the book so that they could see the pictures. They crowded around her and leaned against her and put their hands on her shoulders. They were completely still when she read, still and listening. After the reading she told them that her voice was tired and it was time to read her own book to herself. She selected a

copy of *Great Expectations* and opened it to the chapter where she had left off. Before long, Mariah was as lost in her book as the children had been in theirs. When she looked up at the clock, she couldn't believe how the time had flown. She had surely found peace and pleasure in this quiet place. After the hurly-burly of her life at home and at school, it was nothing short of miraculous.

"Library's closing," Mrs. Phipps called. Mariah put on her jacket. Mrs. Phipps came over to her. "Thanks for being such a help, Mariah. You really saved my life today. I hope you'll come whenever you can and give me a hand. You're very good at it. Maybe tomorrow we can have a talk."

Walking home, Mariah realized that no talk would help. There were tough times ahead. She began to wonder about how she had gotten herself into such a lot of trouble. She had done it all by herself. She couldn't blame anybody; that was for sure. No one had pushed her into making a lending library. It was completely her own idea. It had seemed such a great idea, too. She could never in a million years have predicted that all these troubles would grow out of it. The fact that they had, shook Mariah to her toes. Her confidence was shot. She had gone too far and she hadn't known it till it was too late. The people she had taken for granted most, her parents, were miserable, and the people she thought she could trust, her classmates, were not dependable. She had miscalculated. It was very unlike Mariah to think and think about things she had done. Usually she just went ahead and did something new. But this Lending Library was different, or maybe she was changing. She couldn't think of doing something new. She was in too much trouble and she would have to keep facing up to it until it was over. Somehow the library had helped her. It was a good place to get in touch with your thoughts and get some distance from outside problems and pressures. But those problems still existed, and they had to be dealt with.

Irwin was the only Delany at home. He was working on his second bunch of bananas with his face only inches out of a large book in Latin.

"Hi," Mariah said.

"Pinkwater called; said to call her right back." He didn't look up for a minute.

On the telephone Pinkwater sounded teary. "Listen, Mariah, nobody pays any attention when I tell them to bring back their books. They laugh at me, and they're beginning to detest you. Some people say, 'If she wants them let her come and get them.'"

"Okay then, that's what I'll have to do."

"Good," Pinkwater said and sighed with relief.

"And I want you to come with me."

"Oh Mariah, I can't do that."

"You can and you will and we start at Dave Peterson's tomorrow morning."

"Oh, but Dave gift wrapped his . . . uh."

"So he's the one," Mariah said triumphantly. "Thank you very much."

"Oh dear," Emma wailed.

Mariah slammed down the telephone. Finks and traitors surrounded her. Her path was set, even though her course would be rough. She had gotten into this thing and somehow she'd get out of it. No matter what.

11

The next morning, which was Saturday, Mariah Delany, short, round, and pale, stood beside Emma Pinkwater, tall, skinny, and stooped, outside the door of Dave Peterson's apartment, number 14D. Mariah was ringing the bell. Her green eyes fixed on the penciled name card stuck to the door just below its peephole.

TAMARA PETERSON

DEALER IN RARE AND ANTIQUE BOOKS

Beneath this namecard was a large colorful poster decorated with flowers, curlicues, and balloons. It said, "Welcome to the Petersons' Glorious Fifteenth Anniversary Bash."

It took forever till Dave opened the door, and when he saw Mariah he began to close it, but she slipped herself into the foyer and Pinkwater followed. The foyer was festooned with crèpe paper, which was looped from wall to chandelier, creating a tent ceiling. A metal clothes rack was pushed to one side. Through the archway Mariah could see into the living room where party preparations were going on. Folding chairs

lay stacked on the floor, card tables leaned against the wall, and on a long wooden shelf was a pile of gaily wrapped gifts with anniversary cards opened for display behind them. Mrs. Peterson was going back and forth from the living room to the kitchen, just behind it, setting up a table for drinks.

"What do you want?" Dave scratched his ear and looked nervously into the living room.

"You know what I want and I'm not leaving till I get it."

"Then I guess you've come to live with us."

"What's that supposed to mean?"

"It means . . . Look, Mariah," Dave suddenly changed his mood from annoyance to humble distress. "I told you I'd replace the book with a brand-new paperback because the one I borrowed from you is lost."

"Where?"

"If I knew, it wouldn't be . . ."

"Okay, let me help you find it." She started past him but he hopped backward and blocked her way.

"It's not here and this isn't the way libraries work," he informed her. "If you lose a book from the Public Library, they let you replace it with another copy."

"My library doesn't work that way," Mariah said. "Anyway how do you know it's not here? You told me it was lost."

Dave looked into the living room nervously. "I lost it someplace else."

At that moment Mariah was certain that the book was on the gift-laden shelf in the living room, gift-wrapped and awaiting presentation to Mr. and Mrs. Peterson. She guessed it was Dave's dumb way of giving his folks an impressive anniversary present for practically nothing. She had to think up some way to examine the stack of gift-wrapped packages.

"David," Mrs. Peterson called from the living room. "We need you to come in and help."

"Okay." He stood uncomfortably on one foot, not wanting to leave the foyer.

"Go ahead," said Mariah. "We'll just wait for you right here."

"Uh, I'd rather you didn't," Dave said.

"David." Mrs. Peterson appeared in the archway. "Why hello, girls. I didn't realize you were here. I'd ask you in, but as you can see we're setting up for the big bash." She giggled. "Oh well, I suppose the girls could join you in the kitchen for a fast soda, David."

"No, Ma." Dave waved awkwardly. "It's not that kind of visit."

"Oh, uh-huh." Mrs. Peterson's mind was now on something else. "Then finish up and you can come help us open the chairs and tables."

"We'd be happy to help out," Mariah said. "Me and Pinkwater we'd love to help."

She forged after Mrs. Peterson, dragging Pinkwater behind her.

"Aren't you sweet."

"Aw, please don't," Dave followed, protesting weakly. But it was too late. Mariah had begun to unfold the rented chairs that were piled on the floor.

"Come on, Emma. Grab a chair."

In no time the entire bunch of chairs were unfolded and arranged around the sides of the long living room.

"You're very kind." Mrs. Peterson smiled. "I don't know what your business with David was, but you've certainly helped me out."

"My business with Dave," Mariah said, "is, he borrowed a book from my Lending Library and never returned it."

"Oh, I *am* sorry," said Mrs. Peterson.

"I told her I'd replace it," Dave said.

"Good boy," said his mother proudly.

"But that won't do," said Mariah. "The original is very valuable."

Dave had begun to walk them back to the foyer.

"Valuable?" Mrs. Peterson looked amused. "You know, dear, valuable books are my business and there aren't all that many of them. What did it look like, this valuable book?"

"It was covered in leather," said Mariah, her eyes sweeping the pile of gifts on the shelf in the living room. "Dark, rich-looking leather."

"Mmmm-hmm." Mrs. Peterson nodded.

Mariah knew as certainly as she had ever known anything in her life that the book was there on that heap in the living room, probably the sloppy-looking package with the dirty wool bow, a real Dave Peterson job if she ever saw one. The question was how to get her hands on it. "It had dark brown leather corners and the spine was brown too," Mariah went on describing and stalling for time, struggling for an inspiration. "Actually, Dave told me you had seen it and said it wasn't worth much."

"I said that?" Mrs. Peterson looked confused. "Well, so many things happen around here, I just don't remember. Now I must go back inside, I have so much to do. Good-by, dears, you've been sweet to help." She waved and returned to the kitchen.

What to do now? Mariah gripped her hands together behind her back. It seemed they would have to leave. Dave had opened the door for them. His mother had said good-by. Mariah couldn't think of a solitary reason to prolong the visit, when Pinkwater, starting her nervous, gawky trek across the foyer, and not noticing a chair stacked with boxes of crèpe paper, stumbled over it, sprawling on the floor between the overturned box and the upset chair.

Trust Pinkwater. The idea came to Mariah in a flash. "Emma," she cried. "It's happening to you."

"Huh?" Pinkwater started to get up, but Mariah pushed her back down.

"Stay there, you know your doctor told you not to move when it starts."

"What starts?" Dave whinnied.

"Her fits. She has fits. Oh Lord." Mariah appealed to the ceiling.

Pinkwater was struggling to get up, but Mariah sat on her chest.

"Hey, Mariah," Pinkwater howled. "Get off of me."

"See, she's losing control. She goes crazy, doesn't remember anything."

"What thing?" Pinkwater screamed.

"Fits, you lunatic," Mariah bellowed into her face. Oh, why couldn't she be working with Coopersmith? Coopersmith would have understood immediately.

"Fits?" Pinkwater asked.

"Get your mother in here, Dave. Please. She'll know what to do. Hurry. I can't restrain Pinkwater all day. She gets violent and is very strong."

Dave ran out of the foyer, through the living room and into the kitchen. He was gone just long enough for Mariah to inform Pinkwater of her fits. By the time Dave rushed in with Mrs. Peterson behind him, Pinkwater was doing a first-class fit. Flailing the air with her long arms and legs, she let her head roll crazily from side to side. She also made weird noises.

"I can't stand it." Mariah wept and pulled back just as it seemed Pinkwater would strike her.

Mrs. Peterson looked at the girl on the floor. It seemed as if any minute she might join her in a fit of her own. "Oh, my God," she said over and over.

"I'll get her some water," Mariah said. She ran out of the foyer, made a bee line to the gift table, seized the sloppily-wrapped package, and tore it open. Victory. *Great Expectations*.

In the foyer, Mrs. Peterson and Dave were attempting to approach Pinkwater by grabbing at her wheeling limbs.

"Fit's over," Mariah cried, holding the book up in the air.

Mrs. Peterson stood up, Pinkwater stood up. "I beg your pardon, my dear," Mrs. Peterson said cooly. "You are making an outrageous accusation and I demand that you return my book. That is a present from Dave and his sister, an anniversary present. It does not belong to you." She reached out and snatched the book from Mariah's grasp.

Mariah tugged back, but Mrs. Peterson had the book clasped firmly against her chest.

"David and his sister have chosen a beautiful gift for me. I won't let you spoil it."

"It's mine and and my father's," said Mariah.

"It's mine and a beauty." Mrs. Peterson smiled at Dave and opened the book. "A truly wonderful editionnnnn." She gazed at the first page. Mariah watched her eyes grow frighteningly large. Written across the page in black Magic Marker was PROPERTY OF THE MARIAH DELANY LENDING LIBRARY.

"DAVID!" Mrs. Peterson gasped.

Mariah took this opportunity to grab the book from her limp hand, shove her limp son out of the way, and beat it. Pinkwater moved speedily behind her. As they ran down the corridor toward the elevator, they heard "David, I *am* disappointed," followed by, "I didn't think it was so serious. I said I'd replace it."

"The dope didn't even have the brains to tear out the title page," Mariah hooted once they were out on the sidewalk and laughing so they could hardly breathe.

Mariah stopped laughing. She remembered that she hadn't had the brains to tear out the title page either before returning the book to her father's shelf. She remembered that she too had somehow taken books that didn't really belong to her and then she actually felt a wave of sympathy for David Peterson of apartment 14D.

12

The story of the return of *Great Expectations* spread through school the following Monday with embellishments, exaggerations, and twists until it acquired some of the proportions of a folk tale. Mariah and Emma were heroines of the tale, and no one gave either of them any trouble that day. Mariah was treated with a kind of awed respect that was new to her. Pinkwater was proud to be known as the first Collecting Agent. Several people came up to

Mariah to ask if the Lending Library would be open for returns later that day.

After school Mariah went home to wait. It wasn't long before the doorbell started to ring and books began to pile up on her desk. When the last book was turned in, its borrower, little Enid Lucton, peered over the top of Mariah's desk and said, "Oh, Miss Librarian, where do I go to take out a new book?"

Mariah leaned forward and took Enid's round face in her two hands. "The Mariah Delany Lending Library is officially closed," she said slowly and with emphasis. "Forever."

"Oh." Enid sighed. "I liked the cocoa."

Mariah made her some in celebration. Then she checked each and every card against the books and replaced every book lovingly upon its proper shelf or stack. She put *Best Desserts in the World* back in the kitchen and washed her hands. Its cover was sticky.

When Gertrude and Henry Delany returned from work late in the afternoon, Mariah wordlessly produced the shoebox full of cards, each one marked RETURNED.

"Does this mean that they're all back, Mariah?" asked her mother.

"Yes," Mariah said. "You can check them."

"We don't have to," Henry Delany said. "We have always trusted your abilities as far as your enterprises are concerned, Mariah. When you told us that the books would come back, we knew they would. You'd find a way if anyone could."

The Delanys sat down to dinner. Mariah was very proud of herself in a subdued sort of way. After dinner her mother noticed a far-off look in her daughter's green eyes.

"Oh, Mariah, you have that look. I think you're planning a new venture."

"No," Mariah said.

"Mariah dear, I know you," was all Mrs. Delany said, but those few words were all that were needed. Mariah knew by heart the rest of the words and the feelings behind them. In spite of this and in spite of everything she had just been through, she knew her mother's fears were justified. Mariah was hatching a new plan.

"Mariah, please remember," Mrs. Delany pleaded softly, over her bowl of pudding.

"I do, I do," Mariah said. But even as she

said it the new plan was at work within her. After dinner Mariah went to her room. She remembered her vow and gratefully did every last bit of homework before she read a few chapters in *Great Expectations*.

The next day Mariah's teachers were delighted by the carefully completed homework she turned in. It was a good day. By the end of her last class Mariah was in a fever of impatience to begin her new enterprise. She grabbed her books, ran down the steps, and raced toward the corner. Pinkwater and Coopersmith followed at her heels. They were running, and calling breathlessly, "Hey, wait up, Delany."

She stood impatiently. Couldn't they tell she was in a big hurry and didn't have all day?

"Delany." Pinkwater gasped, clutching her sides. "We just wondered, what's your new business? We want to be included."

"I can't include you."

"Oh Mariah, puh-lease . . ." Coopersmith wailed. "Don't keep us out."

"Sorry." She started to cross the street.

"You couldn't have done the Lending Library without me," Pinkwater reminded her.

"I know, and thanks."

"Harmonicas wouldn't have gotten off

the ground if I hadn't helped," Cooper-smith piped up. They were walking three abreast, and fast.

"C'mon, Mariah, include us."

"No."

"Well tell us where you're going, or we'll follow you."

Mariah stopped right in the middle of the sidewalk. Pinkwater and Coopersmith lurched to a halt. "I said no more enter-prises. I'm through. I got into too much trouble with the last one. I don't need that kind of trouble."

"But the way you're hurrying, you look like you're on to something."

"I am."

"Well?" they chorused triumphantly. "Where are you going?"

"I'm going to the Public Library."

"Oh yeah." Disappointment.

There was a moment of silence and then Coopersmith said to Pinkwater, "Do you want to come to my place for TV?"

"Okay." Pinkwater eyed Mariah. "You coming too?"

"I told you, I'm going to the library."

Unable to contain herself for another minute, Pinkwater blurted, "Mariah Delany, whatever for?"

"Because it's got everything," Mariah said.

Pinkwater was suspicious, but Coopersmith shrugged. They said good-by.

Mariah began to skip and then, whistling tunelessly, she ran down the remaining streets and up the block and then the stairs. She thought of all the things she had to do. She had to shelve at least two carts of books, read out loud to a bunch of kids, and help arrange a display case. Then, if she was lucky, there would be time to read a few more chapters of *Great Expectations*.

The Public Library was the best enterprise she had ever thought up. It *did* have everything. It was a friendly place, the people were nice, there were interesting jobs to do that really desperately needed doing. Mariah's work was terribly important. Of course, there wasn't any money in the library, but then she didn't have to make an investment, or hoodwink anybody, or make enemies, or get into awful hot water; and after her last experience all this seemed very good. And of course there were all those books to browse among. Yes, it was a great relief, Mariah decided, to be part of the system, the public library system.